BLOOD GONE COLD

KATY GRANT

WEST 44 BOOKS™

Please visit our website, www.west44books.com.
For a free color catalog of all our high-quality books,
call toll free 1-800-398-2504.

Cataloging-in-Publication Data
Names: Grant, Katy.
Title: Blood gone cold / Katy Grant.
Description: Buffalo, NY : West 44, 2025. | Series: West 44
YA verse
Identifiers: ISBN 9781978597396 (pbk.) | ISBN
9781978597389 (library bound) | ISBN 9781978597402
(ebook)
Subjects: LCSH: Sibling rivalry--Juvenile fiction. | Sisters-
-Juvenile fiction. | Siblings--Juvenile fiction. | Burglary--
Juvenile fiction.
Classification: LCC PZ7.1.G766 Bl 2025 | DDC [F]--dc23

First Edition

Published in 2025 by
Enslow Publishing LLC
2544 Clinton Street
Buffalo, New York 14224

Editor: Caitie McAneney
Designer: Tanya Dellaccio Keeney

Photo Credits: Cover (cabin) Sean Jorg/Shutterstock.com;
series background Kichigin/Shutterstock.com.

Printed in the United States of America

CPSIA compliance information: Batch #CS25W44: For further information contact
Enslow Publishing LLC at 1-800-398-2504.

Find us on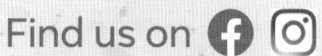

For Pat,
my biggest booster

And for Mandi and Rachel,
thanks for the inspiration!

SNOWBOARDING

Sun low in the sky.
Shadows long.
In the shade,
the snow is blue.
Last run of the day.

      Slopes so beautiful.
      So white.
      So perfect.

Breathe in the cold air.

      Point
      my
      board
      straight
      downhill.

Have to make this a good run.
DON'T overthink!
Feel it.

Board flat,
going fast.

Too fast?

I put pressure
on my heels,
then toes.

Heel side, toe side.
Rocking my edges.
Controlling my speed.

Is this okay?
I think so.

I'm back on my heels when
my board starts ch-ch-chattering.

I catch an edge and—

2

BAM!

I bail big-time.

MY SISTER

I hit
the packed snow
so hard.
I try to sit up.

Oh, great.

Natalie's

carving

down

the

mountain.

She sprays snow in my face
as she stops.
Lifts her goggles.
Raises an eyebrow.

"Nice biff."

Lowers her goggles.

Gives me a princess wave.
Turns her board and
glides down the mountain.

My sister.

Eight long months.
Then she leaves
for college.

I can't wait till
I'm an only child.

SIBLING RIVALRY

Our parents wait at the base
of the mountain.
Skis propped on their shoulders.
Nat's with them,
her board under her arm.

      "Abby, over here!" Dad yells to me.

      "Honey, are you okay?" says Mom.
      "Natalie said
      you had a terrible wipeout."

I unstrap my bindings.
"I just fell. No big deal."

Natalie loves that
she's better than me.
Tells me I think too much.

So what? Thinking gets me
good grades.

We head for
the parking lot.
Pile our gear
in the back of the car
and on the roof rack.

Dad cranks up the heat.
Eases into the
massive traffic jam.

Everyone's leaving
the mountain
at the same time.

Nat and I argue
about dinner.

I want takeout.

                She wants to eat in.

I want junk food.

                She wants healthy.

I flick melting snow at her.

                She kicks me
                when I won't stop.

Suddenly, Mom hits
the dashboard
with both fists.

"THAT'S ENOUGH!"

8

LUCKY GIRLS

Mom turns around in her seat.
Shakes the dreaded mom finger
at us.
The lecture starts.

About how lucky we are.
About how hard Dad and she work.
Which I admit is true.

Mom's a real estate agent.
Dad has his own roofing business.

Mom grew up in the Philippines.
Moved here in her 20s.
Married white-guy Dad.
Now they're living the dream.

But her kids give her nightmares.

"Family is everything.
You two should be
best friends.

We have a weekend
in the mountains, but
you're ruining it!

Here's the dinner plan.
We're going out.
You two are
on your own."

ON OUR OWN

Mom got that right.
We'll be on our own
for sure.

Natalie is so bored
hanging out with
just me.

Me, the nerd
who can't get enough
science facts.
Who works
math problems
for fun.

Nat is always
with her friends
or going out with
her latest guy.

She thinks
I'm weird.
I actually like
being alone.

I think
she's shallow
for caring about
being popular.

So
on our own
sounds good
to me.

WEEKEND GETAWAY

The cabin where
we're staying is
cute and cozy.

Way outside of
town.
Tucked away among
tall pine trees.

Very wooded
and private.
Thick snow
blankets the ground.

Steps lead to
a wooden porch
with two rocking chairs.
Stone chimney on one side.
Hot tub out back.

An agent Mom knows
owns this place but
hardly ever uses it.

We lug our gear
into the garage.

Mom and Dad head to
the downstairs bedroom.
Nat goes upstairs.

I go to the kitchen
and make some ramen.
I'm still sore
from my wipeout.

Time for the hot tub!

WICKED

Climbing the stairs,
I hear Natalie in the shower.
See clothes piled
on the bedroom floor.

I find Natalie's phone
in her snowpants pocket.

A wicked smile spreads
across my face.

A night without texting
her million friends
will seriously
kill her!

Nat's always teasing me
that I think a lot
but I never *do* anything.

So I decide fast
to do something.

TORTURING
MY SISTER

I race downstairs.
Look around.

Bookshelves beside the fireplace.
Stacks of games and puzzles
on one shelf.

I switch her phone to silent.
Grab a puzzle box.
Open the lid.
Pop her phone inside.

Just then, I hear
Mom and Dad.
I leap to the couch.

      Just lying there,
      innocent.

Mom and Dad have
showered and dressed.
Mom brushes her long, black hair.
Twists it into a loose bun.

She asks if I cleaned the kitchen.
I promise I will.

"Listen, Abby," says Dad.
"Try not to kill each other
while we're gone.
We'll be back by 9:00."

"Okay.
You guys look nice,
by the way.
Have fun!"

I head upstairs
to get my swimsuit on
and get outside.

Before
my sweet sister
discovers
what I did.

That reminds me—
I better hide *my* phone
from *her*.

I turn it to silent and
stick it under the mattress.

I change super-fast,
throw on my hoodie.
Grab a towel
from the downstairs bathroom.

Then I turn off
all the lights.

So all Nat will see
when she gets
out of the shower
is a

dark,

empty

house.

HOT TUB

I open the back door.
The cold like
iceberg breath.

Massive icicles hang off
the edge of the roof.
Glass daggers.

I shiver as
I fumble with the cover.
Buckles on each corner
attach the cover to the hot tub.

I unsnap them.
Brrrr! So cold.

I lift one side of the cover.
It folds in half.
Steam rises from
the water.

The cover is
insulated, heavy.
I try pushing
the folded-up cover off.

But I'm f-f-f-freezing!
So forget it.

Hoodie off,
I climb in.

Ahhhh!
Instant
warmth.

PERFECT NIGHT

Buttons
turn on the light
and jets.

The water churns.
Steam rises.
Soothing my achy body.

Kind of weird to sit here,
half the hot tub uncovered,
the other half covered.

I peek under
the covered half.
See a cave glowing
in blue light.

I look up at the sky.
Deep.
Black.
Endless.

Star

                  star

    star

                           star

A treasure chest full
of a billion diamonds
spilled across the sky.

The brightest star
(it's not a star)
just above
the horizon.

      Venus.

Perfect night.
I could sit here
for-
ever.

PAYBACK

The hot tub cycle ends
and the jets turn off
automatically.

I sigh. Climb out,
dry off fast.

I pull on my hoodie and
fold the cover back.
Snap all the buckles closed.

I head to the back door,
turn the knob,
but

it doesn't budge.

It's locked.

Of course.

I'm wet.
It's freezing.
It's dark.

Forget what Dad said.

I

am going

to kill

my sister.

23

HEADLIGHTS

No point knocking.
She won't let me in.

No choice
but to sit
in the hot tub
for hours.

Waiting for
Mom and Dad
to get back.

Either that or freeze.

I unbuckle the straps.
Again.
Fold back half the cover.
Again.

About to pull off my hoodie
when I see it.

Lights shining on the treetops
in the backyard.
I hear the sound of
tires crunching.

A car is pulling up
the driveway.

Yes! I'm saved.
Ha, ha!
Take that, Natalie.

Mom and Dad
are back early.
Must've forgotten
something.

I cross the patio
to the side gate.
It's padlocked.

But I can yell
over the fence.
Tell them
I'm locked out.

I SPY

Two car doors slam shut.
I peek through
the wood slats of the gate.

Driveway
flooded in yellow light.

My blood goes cold.

That's not our car.
Those aren't my parents.

It's two men.

Two scruffy-looking white guys.
Standing beside
a mud-splattered pickup.

Oh. My. God.

What the—?

TWO STRANGE MEN

My heart pounds
bomp bomp bomp.
Caged animal
in my chest.

I press my eye against the
gap in the wood slats.
My bare legs won't
stop shaking.

One guy:
      taller
      pudgy
      gray coat
      trucker hat.

Other guy:
      smaller
      stringy hair
      black jacket
      goatee.

He drags on
a cigarette.
Nods toward the cabin.

I LISTEN, BREATHLESS

"Nice, huh? How's this
for a place to crash?"

        "You sure it's empty?"
        asks Trucker Hat.

"Yep. Checked it out
last week.
Owners are some
rich snobs. Only come up
couple of times a year."

Goatee takes a long drag,
flips the butt away.
"It's all ours!"

I suck in cold air.

Remember how I
turned off
all the lights.

Except Natalie has
the light on
in the bedroom.

But
that room is
in the back.

So
all they see is a
dark,
empty
cabin.

They talk some more.
About the light
flooding the driveway.
Motion sensor.

About the driveway being plowed.
Goatee says don't worry.
Owners of these vacation cabins
pay a plow service.

Goatee swears he
checked the place out.

"Come on. Let's
go inside."

GO INSIDE?

Go inside?
They can't
go inside!

"Which way in?" asks Trucker Hat.

"Around back.
So nobody sees us.
The gate's locked.
We'll have to
climb over."

They crunch through
the snow
heading
toward the gate.

Heading
toward me.

I've got to hide!

TRAPPED!

I run across the patio
on tiptoes,
trying not to make
a sound.

I look around.
The fence pens
me in.

Nowhere to hide.
I'm trapped!
They'll catch me!

Stop. Think.
Use your brain.

I see it!
My only hope.

UNDERWATER

The hot tub steams
in the dark night.
Half uncovered.

I hear them
at the gate.
Struggling to
climb over.

I shuck off my hoodie.
Roll it and my towel
in a tight ball.
Toss them
out of sight.

Hear one thump,
then another
(they're over the gate)
as I sink into
black water.

Grab the sides
of the cover.
Pull it slowly closed
over my head
as heavy boots
clomp toward me.

HIDDEN

Submerged.
Underwater.
Holding my breath.

Water
so warm.

Open my eyes.
Pitch black.
All sounds muffled.

I am hidden.
Safe!

    For now.

BREATHE

I float on my back
face up.
Feel my face above water.
Open my mouth and

breathe.

I can breathe!

A five-inch space
between the cover
and the waterline
lets me breathe.

NOW WHAT?

What will they do?
I breathe slowly
in and out.

The air is steamy.
The clean smell of
chemicals
rises from the water.

I hear them
walk past me.
Hear their
muffled voices.
Can't hear
their words.

Thank God Natalie
locked the door.

BREAKING GLASS

A crash.
The sharp tinkle of
breaking glass.

They've broken in!

In my head
I see the kitchen door.
The upper half
of glass panels.

Break one out,
reach in and
turn the locks.
Just like that,
they're inside.

Natalie!
Two men,
they just broke in!

I yell psychic messages
in my head.

Call 911!

BUT WAIT . . .

She can't call
911
because
I hid her phone.
And
I hid *my* phone.

So
she's trapped
upstairs.
And these
two sleazy guys
will find her
and . . .

Natalie!

We're sisters.
Okay, so we don't
always
get along,
especially lately.

But
we're sisters.
We're bonded
by blood.
Sometimes we know
what the other is
thinking.

Natalie!

Hide!

CAN'T LET THEM

They're inside now.
I feel so sick
I may puke.

Panicked, I float
in the safest
hiding spot
in the world.

I breathe in
air
as moist as a
wet sponge.

They will never
find me
here.

But I
can't let them
find
my sister.

GATHER DATA

I have to assess
the situation.
Gather data.
I have to see
what's going on.

I have to
leave my
hiding spot.

I lift the cover oh-so
slowly.
Gulp in frosty air.
Step soundlessly
out of the water.
Ease the cover
closed.

Still flushed and warm
from the hot water,
I feel for my towel
and hoodie.

I find them
where I tossed them
at the edge
of the patio.

Then I creep oh-so
slowly
to the window.

DISCOVERY

I dry off with the towel,
then pull on my hoodie.
Tuck my short, black hair
inside the warm hood.

Barefoot,
I watch out for
broken glass.
I peek in
the kitchen window.

Lights are on now.
Past the kitchen,
I see them in the
living room.

Trucker Hat is talking,
waving his arms.
Goatee is shaking his head.
Both of them are
freaking out.

They see
all our stuff.

Dirty dishes
in the kitchen.

Wet socks and
boots by the door.

Now they know
their new digs
aren't empty.

Now they'll start
looking
for whoever
might be
here.

AT LEAST

At least Nat is
out of sight.

*Natalie, find
someplace
to hide!*

By now she's
heard them,
right?

The sound of
men's voices.
The smell of
stinking cigarettes.

By now she's
seen the lights
downstairs,
right?

MAYBE

Maybe she's found
the second-best
hiding spot
in the world.

Maybe I can stay
outside,
out of sight.

Maybe Mom and Dad will
be back anytime now.
They'll see the strange truck
and save us.

Or.

Maybe I
should be the one
to
save us.

OKAY, THINK

What should I
do?

"Use your brain.
It's your greatest
strength."

That's what
Dad always says.

So *think*.
Figure this out.
Analyze the situation.
Formulate a plan.

THE FACTS

1. It's two against two.

2. Two grown men.

3. Two teenage girls.

4. They look like they are twice our size.

5. They are bigger, stronger, meaner. They will figure out fast that no adults are around.

6. This far out of town, there's no help close by.

7. Advantage: they don't have weapons. (I hope.)

8, Advantage: they don't know I'm out here.

9. Advantage: I'm smarter than these two clown hats.

THIS CHANGES EVERYTHING

I stand here,
bare feet turning
into blocks of ice.
I'm looking in
the window,
      thinking
      not acting.

Goatee rushes into
the kitchen.
I step back
out of sight.
Darkness is
my shield.

Outside in the dark,
it's easy to look
into a lighted room.

In a lighted room,
it's almost impossible
to see anything
outside in the dark.

I watch Goatee pull
open drawers.
Rummage around.

I see him grab something
shiny.
Go back to the
living room.

The something shiny
is a
knife.

A big psycho
knife.

He stomps upstairs
carrying that
big psycho
knife.

This changes
everything.

WHERE IS SHE?

Shaking hard,
I picture Goatee searching
the upstairs rooms.

Walking through the loft,
past the pool table,
the foosball table.

Past the puffy couch,
the puffy armchair,
the giant flatscreen.

Into the room
with the bunk beds.
Where I slept
on the bottom
like some little kid.

Into the room
with the comfy bed.
Where Natalie slept
like some queen.

Where is she hiding?
Closet?
Under a bed?

In the shower
with the curtain
closed?

Not in the shower!
Not in the shower!

That really is
Psycho.

FOOTSTEPS

While I've been imagining,
Trucker Hat's been pacing.

He hears something,
looks up.
I press close to
the window.

Faint footsteps
come down the stairs.
I see Natalie first.
In yoga pants and
hoodie.

Behind her is Goatee
gripping her wrists.
Holding them
behind her back
with one hand.

In his other hand
he holds the knife
to her face.
Its sharp point
brushes through her
long, dark hair.

Oh, God!
Oh, no!

My sister!
They have my
sister!

PURE EVIL

Goatee lets out
a laugh.
Loud enough
for me to hear.

It sounds like
pure evil.

An evil
that makes me feel cold.

For a
split second
I think,

I should rush in!
Grab a
kitchen chair
and charge them.

Hold them off
till we can
get away.

Run out the
front door
and escape.

HUGE ADVANTAGE

I stop myself.
Be smart.
Be logical.
Don't make any
wrong moves.

I still have
one advantage.

A HUGE
advantage.

They don't know
I'm out here.

They're thinking
it's two against one.

They're sizing up
Natalie and thinking
they got this
under control.

They don't have
all the facts.
But I do.

I have to use that.

Because if I don't,
we could both
end up captives.

NAT'S MESSAGE

Suddenly I hear
Nat's voice
loud and clear:

"You better get out of here!
My family just went
to the gas station.

They'll be back
any minute.
My dad has guns!
So does my brother."

She's talking loud
and I'm thinking,
Huh?

Guns?
A brother?
We don't have
either.

But then—oh!
I get it!

She's sending me
a message
loud and clear.

She knows
I'm out here
waiting
to save her.

54

STOP THEM

"Shut up!"
yells Goatee.
He's gripping her hands
behind her back.

He bends her arm up,
twisting it,
hurting her.

She makes a face,
but she doesn't
make a sound.

She won't give him
the satisfaction
of knowing
he hurt her.

He and Trucker Hat
talk, argue.
I can't hear
their words.

Then Goatee pushes
Natalie toward the door.

She yells, "Wait!
At least let me get
my coat and shoes on."

They're leaving!

And they're taking Natalie
with them.

Unless . . .

TAKING ACTION

Suddenly I'm
running,
taking action.

Bare feet racing
across the frozen patio.
The side gate is locked!

I need to climb over.
I scramble up on the
big, black trash can.

I swing my legs over,
land in the snow
below.

I sink down into
the frozen wetness.
Struggle to
stand up.

Then I'm up.
Running again
toward the
cabin's front door.
Wait—
Motion sensor light!

Don't set it off.
I run behind the pickup
parked in the driveway.
The light stays off.

I can't let them
take Natalie!

Because if they
leave here with her
in that pickup
truck,

I know
I'll never see
my sister
again.

WEAPON

Running,
stumbling,
bare feet
through
deep snow.

The front door
is still closed.

When they
come out that door,
I can't fight them.
I have to take them
by surprise.

Weapon!
I need a weapon!
Tree branch?
Rock?

Running up to the
front porch,
I see them.

A whole arsenal!
Hanging off the
roof edge.

Glass daggers.

Sharp enough

to stab,

to pierce,

to hurt.

DAGGER DRAWN

Up the porch steps,
standing on tiptoes,
I reach overhead.

Break off a giant
icicle.
Grip it in
both hands.

I press my back
against the cabin wall
beside the door and

I wait.

Glass dagger drawn.

ATTACK

Over the drumbeat
of my thrumming heart
I hear muffled voices
just inside the door.

Then—
the door opens.
A patch of light
falls on wooden boards
of the porch.

Nat comes out first,
Goatee next,
Trucker Hat in back.

"AHHHHHH!"

I roar like a lioness
pouncing on prey.
Stabbing!
Slashing!

Hearing screams, yells,
some mine,
some not.

Icicle shatters.
Need another weapon!
Grab a rocking chair,
shove it
into knees.

I'm yelling at
Natalie to run to
the woods where
they can't see us.

My words
sound strange,
but there's

no time to think.

Natalie grabs me
and we're leaping
off the porch,
heading for the
giant pine trees.

Running
        tripping
                falling.

Disappearing into
darkness.

SO RELIEVED

The darkness
swallows us
and we're
in the trees.
The clean scent of pine
fills my nostrils.

Natalie hugs me,
her warm breath
tickling my cheek.

"Abby! Oh, my God!
I knew you were
out there on the patio
watching.

I knew you'd
figure out
some way to
save me!
I just knew it!"

"Shhh! Keep your
voice down so
they don't hear us."

Hugging her,
I feel
so relieved.
She's here.
She's safe.
We're together.

TAGALOG

Natalie pulls away,
looks at me.
I see her smiling
in the dim light.

> "I can't believe
> you spoke Tagalog!"
> she whispers.
> "That was so
> smart of you!"

I stare at her,
confused.
"I did? Really?"

> "Yes! When you told me
> to run to the woods!
> So they wouldn't know
> what you were saying."

I can't believe
I spoke Tagalog.
Didn't plan it.
Must have just
blurted it out.

We don't really speak
our mother's first language.
But we've heard her
and all our Filipino family
speak it our whole lives.

I laugh softly.
I don't always
understand how
my brain works.

Sometimes
I surprise
myself.

BRILLIANT

We stumble through
the snow.
I'm glad I'm used to
running.
This year I did
cross-country.

Not that I'm
an athlete.
I just wanted to
look good on
college applications.

"What did you
hit them with?" Nat whispers.
"I heard them yell,
but I jumped off that porch
so fast I couldn't see."

"I stabbed the guy
who had you with
an icicle.
Then I shoved
the rocking chair
into the other guy."

"Wow! Wow!
You stabbed him
with an icicle?
That's so brilliant!"

She starts laughing.
"I can't believe it!"

"Hey, I had to use
any weapon I
could find."

"No, I mean I
can't believe
you actually
did something.

I was worried you
had fifteen different
plans in mind.

I pictured you out there
analyzing them,
trying to decide
which one."

Normally, it annoys me
when Nat points out my flaws.
But I just laugh.
"It only takes a
life-or-death situation
to get me moving!"

MAZE

"Look!" I point to two
pinpoints of light
behind us in the distance,
close to the ground.

       "The flashlights from their
       cell phones!" Natalie says.

"They must be
looking for our tracks
in the snow.
We have to keep
moving."

We weave in and out
of the trees,
backtracking,
crisscrossing.

We make a maze
of footprints to
try to throw them off.

At least the snow is
not so deep here.
Tree branches overhead
keep it from drifting.

We're running and weaving.
We don't dare stop to look
behind us.

I run like Trucker Hat is
breathing down
my neck.
I run like Goatee is
coming at me
with a knife.

NINJA

I hear Natalie behind me
giggling.
We're running for
our lives,
and she won't stop
laughing.

"What's so funny?"
I hiss.

"You are," she says.

"Stabbing men
with icicles.
Throwing rocking chairs
at them.
Speaking a foreign language.
And now throwing them
off our trail."

"What's funny
about that?"

"I had no idea!
My sister's a
ninja!"

I can't help it.
I start laughing, too.

Must be the adrenaline.

71

FREEZING

Finally, we stop,
suck in icy cold air,
and look back.

"I don't see their lights now,"
Natalie says. She lets out
a slow sigh.

I peer into the
black night.
"I don't see them, either.
But that doesn't mean
they're not out there
somewhere.

We can't stop until
we're someplace
safe."

Nat looks at me.
"Ab, you must be
freezing!"

I look down
at my bare legs,
bare feet
buried in the snow.

My feet are
so cold, it makes
the backs of
my knees ache.

My hood still
covers my head.
I pull the drawstrings
tighter.

Shove my hands
into the handwarmer
pocket.

"I'm okay.
As long as
we keep moving."

What I don't say is
I can't feel my feet
at all now.

What I don't say is
I wonder if
I have frostbite.

WHO WERE THOSE GUYS?

We keep crunching through
the snow, putting distance
between us and them.

Finally, I ask
what I've been
wondering all along.

"Nat, who were
those guys?
Why did they break in
in the first place?"

> She shakes her head.
> "I have no idea.
> When I heard
> the glass break,
> I thought you broke
> the window.
>
> Then I heard men's voices.
> Freaked me out so bad!
> I crept out to the loft
> so I could hear."

"They were talking about
crashing there.
'For as long as we want,'
I heard them say.

They were talking about
stuff they could steal
to sell later.

That's when they
figured out people
were staying there.

One of them
just wanted
to leave—"

"That was the one
in the trucker hat,"
I say.

"The other said
they were in this
too deep.
Sounds like
they're on the run.

He's the one who
came upstairs and
grabbed me."

GREAT
HIDING PLACE

"Where were you hiding,
by the way?"

"I squeezed into
the bathroom cabinet.
It was empty."

"Really? That's a
great hiding place!"

"It was perfect except
my hair was sticking out.
That's how he
found me."

LIKE SISTERS

Natalie and I both
had long hair
when we were little.

I cut mine short
when high school started.
I wanted my own look.
Different from Nat.

Her hair is still
long, black,
glossy, beautiful.

We look like sisters.
Petite.
Black hair.
Dark eyes.

People can't tell—
are we Latina?
Native American?
Asian?

We have white girl names.
Natalie and Abby Miller.
But
people just don't know,
so

we keep them
guessing.
And that makes me
laugh.

PROUD

I'm a proud
Filipina American.

Proud of my
Asian heritage.

If people ask
my ethnicity,
I tell them.

But some people
can be horrible.

Like the old man who
slowed down his car
and yelled at me
as I walked home
from the bus stop.

      "Go back to China!"

"Shut up, you stupid jerk!"
I yelled back
as he sped off.

I can be shy, quiet,
but
don't be hating on
people of color.

I won't
stand for that.

HOT TUB HIDEOUT

I tell Nat about my
hot tub hideout.

I tell her about the
airspace between
the waterline and
the cover.

She stares at me,
amazed.

"Oh, my God!
That's perfect!
They never would've
thought to look there.

You could've
stayed there
all night.
Warm and
out of sight."

"Yeah, it was
perfect.
But I couldn't
stay there.

I couldn't leave you
alone in the cabin
with those creeps."

TOUGH GUY

"Why didn't they
just leave?" I ask.
"Why did they want to
take you with them?"

> "The guy in the hat
> didn't want to
> take me along
> But the smaller guy—
> when he saw me,
> he looked so relieved.
>
> He was suddenly
> this tough guy with a knife
> when he saw I was
> only a teenage girl.
>
> He told the other guy
> I'd seen their faces.
> I'd call the cops
> and describe them.
> So they had to
> take me with them."

"There was no way
I was going to
let that happen," I say.

> Natalie sighs.
> "Thank God.
> It scared me
> to death thinking
> what they might
> do to me."

WARM AND SAFE

"Don't think about
those guys at all!
Think about
something good."

      "Like what?" Natalie asks.
      She sounds annoyed.
      I don't blame her.

What's good about
running away from
two crazy men who
may still be chasing us.

"Think about *last* night," I say.
"Our first night at the cabin.

We watched that
gorgeous sunset
from the porch."

      Natalie smiles.
      "Then we went inside
      and ate lasagna."

"Think about
all of us
in front of the fire.

I had on my
flannel pajama pants
and my fuzzy socks."

I bury my nose
in my hoodie and
breathe in.

"Nat! Smell this.
It still smells like
woodsmoke."

Nat sniffs my hoodie.
"You're right.
Pretend like
our bellies are full of
lasagna.

Mom and Dad are
sitting on the couch
beside us."

"We're watching the
crackling fire," I say.
"And all of us are
warm and safe."

HOT CHOCOLATE

We're trudging along,
not going as fast now,
but we have to keep moving.

"Once we're safe
I want a huge cup
of hot chocolate," I say.

"With marshmallows?"
asks Natalie.

"Definitely with
marshmallows.
The cup all warm
in my hands.
So chocolatey.
So delicious.

And a blanket
wrapped around
my shoulders."

"I'll keep putting
more logs on the fire,"
says Nat.
"Until we can feel
the heat on our faces."

Nat puts her arm around
my shoulders and it's
warm as any
blanket.

PRETEND LIKE . . .

I start chuckling.
"Hey, when you said,
'Pretend like . . .'
it reminded me of
when we were little."

"You mean the
Cheyenne and Monica game?"
she asks.

I can hear the smile
in her voice.

"That's exactly what
I mean."

We used to pretend like
we were two grown-ups:
Cheyenne (Natalie)
and Monica (me).

Where did we
come up with
those names?
I have no idea.

Cheyenne had amazing adventures.
Cheyenne traveled the world.

Cheyenne
        jumped out of airplanes.
        Scuba dived.
        Raced around on Jet Skis.

Cheyenne was always
chasing criminals.
And catching them.

Monica was a bank president.
(Why did I make my
grown-up self so boring?)
Monica was always
sending Cheyenne money.

I'd talk into my
pretend cell phone
(an old deck of cards):

"I just sent you
nine million dollars, Cheyenne.
That's all you get
till next month."

BACK THEN

Back then,
Nat and I played
together

all
the
time.

We're two years apart
in school, but
she's only 17 months
older than me.

We argued and fought,
but we were
always,
always
together.

Back then,
we each had
our own room,
but every night
we'd trade off.

I'd bring a sleeping bag
and sleep on her floor.
The next night
she'd sleep on mine.

We drove
Mom and Dad crazy.
We'd talk
and talk
and talk
after lights-out.

They kept trying
to separate us,
but we always
snuck back
to be together.

Back then,
Natalie wasn't
just my sister.

She was
my best friend.

I don't know
what happened
to drive us
so far

          apart.

WHAT HAPPENED

What happened was we grew up.

I became

smart, quiet, nerdy.

Invisible to boys.

Unsure about
everything.

Kind of a loner.

Natalie became

crazy popular.

Boy magnet.

Super sure
of herself.

Busy always.

I love

my family.

Math and science.

Being alone with
my laptop

and my thoughts.

Natalie loves

her friends.

Her boyfriends
(she's on
Number Six).

School (she's with
friends *all* day).

Her phone.

We are   so different

we never   hang out

            together.

I'm not okay with that.   But she is.

ACTUAL CRIMINALS

It hurts thinking about
how close we used to be.
I joke to keep
the mood going.

"What would Cheyenne
do right now
to save us?"
I ask.

Natalie laughs.
"She wouldn't be
running away from
the bad guys.

She'd be
chasing *them*.

I just remember
doing a lot of
karate kicks.

It's easy
to fight
pretend bad guys.

Much harder when
you run into
actual criminals."

TOGETHER (NOT)

It's weird, but
I realize that
this is the
most time
Nat and I
have spent
together

in forever.

Even today
on the slopes
when we were
snowboarding
"together"
while Mom and Dad
skied,

we weren't
together.

Not really.

We sat next
to each other
on the lifts.

We did runs
at the same time.

But we weren't
together.

Nat was always
on her phone
unless she was
bombing down
the run.

(And even then
she was doing
video selfies
half the time
to post on social.)

We didn't really talk.
We never really talk.
Not anymore.

There's a distance,
a coldness,
between us.

The thing is:
I've been missing
Natalie
for a long time.

Even though
she's been
right here.

CREEPY

It's been a while
since we saw
their lights
following us.

I look behind us.
Don't see
any lights
anywhere.

"Still no sign
of them back there."

Nat looks over
her shoulder.
"Maybe they
gave up."

"Maybe," I say.

Or maybe . . .

they are
hidden
watching
waiting
for a chance
to attack us.

Creepy.

"Let's keep moving," I say.

OR ELSE

Nat stops dead still.
"What's wrong?" I ask.

    "I'm worried
    about you.
    I'm okay because
    I actually have clothes on.

    How can you still be
    running with no shoes on?"

I shrug.
"I'm okay.
Running all that
cross-country this year
really helped out tonight."

    Natalie snorts.
    "You weren't running barefoot.
    Here—at least wear my shoes
    for a while."

She leans against
the trunk of a
massive pine tree.
Pulls off her
platform high tops
and socks.

"Here—take them."

"No, I'm okay,
really.
I can't even feel
the cold anymore."

Nat throws a
high top at me.
"Shut up!
Put them on
right now.
Or else."

MIGHT AS WELL

Now she's taking off
her coat and
pushing it toward me.

     "Might as well
     take my coat, too."

I don't argue because
she'll throw something
if I do.

I slip into the coat,
already warm
from her wearing it.

I zip it up all the way.
Instantly, I feel warmer.

But then I lean
against the tree
to put on her
socks and shoes.

It feels so weird.
Like I'm putting them
on someone else's feet.

I can't feel my feet,
or any of my toes.

At all.

That
can't
be
good.

INSANE PAIN

We start walking again.
I feel like I'm walking
on stilts.

It's not
the platform shoes.
It's because
I can't feel
anything.

Until after
a few minutes
I start to feel
something.

Pins and needles
doesn't really
describe it.

More like
electric volts
shooting through
my feet.

Oh my god.
It hurts so
much.

The pain
is
insane.

LOST

"Thanks for
the shoes.
And the coat,"
I say.

The coat does help.
The shoes,
not so much.

> "No problem," says Nat.
> She's annoyed.
> Feeling the cold.

> "Abby, where
> are we?
> I mean, seriously!

> It feels like
> we're walking
> in circles."

"We just need to
keep walking till
we get to the road.
Or till we see
another cabin,"
I say.

"But where's
the road?
What if it's
miles away?"

"It's not."

"It might be."

"I don't think so."

But I honestly
don't know.

Because
we kind of
maybe
have been
walking in circles.

"Want to know
what I think?"
I hear the sharp edge
in her voice.

"What?"

"I think
you got us
lost."

WE. COULD. DIE.

I stop in
my tracks.
Nat bumps
right into me.

"*I* got us
lost?
How is this
my fault?"

"*You're* the one
who said we should
make a maze,
throw them off.

Oh, wait!
I have an idea!
Let's check our phones,
figure out where
we are!

Let's call 911!
Call Mom and Dad!

Oh, wait!
You're the one
who stole my phone!"

I knew it
wouldn't last.
Nat and me
together.

Getting along,
helping
each other.

It doesn't take long
till we start to fight.

Then it all
falls apart.

"I didn't *steal* it!
I just . . . hid it.
Temporarily."

> "A lot of good
> that does us now!
> We are lost
> in the woods.
> On a freezing cold night.
>
> We could die
> out here."

Nat's voice goes
from furious to
terrified.

Now she's quiet.
Looking around
at the towering trees
around us.

> "We. Could. Die."

LET ME THINK

"Don't panic!"
I yell
because she's
making *me* panic.

"We have to
stay calm.
Be logical.
Analyze
the situation."

Nat shakes her head.
"No. Forget it.
Let's just pick
a direction and
walk.
Otherwise,
we'll freeze."

She starts off.
Leaving me behind.
"Wait!" I say.
"Just let me think."

I look around.
We are surrounded.
Trees everywhere.
Think.

I can solve
just about anything
if she'll just
let me think.

THAT FEELING

Natalie walks away.
Leaving me behind.
Still furious.
Not trusting me.

But I trust myself
enough to
think this through.

I look up.
See the billions of stars.
And then—

I get that feeling.
That feeling
that comes to me.

During tests.
Working math problems.
Looking at data.
Analyzing figures.

That feeling
where understanding
slowly spreads
through my brain.

Understanding
that spreads like
colored paint
washing over
white canvas.

When I know
I've solved
the problem.

When I see
the solution
in my head.

Clear as
the stars
above.

VENUS

"Natalie, wait!"
I yell.
"Venus!
We have to find
Venus!"

I run to catch up
to her.

"If we find
Venus
we'll know
where we are."

GO WEST

Natalie stops.
Looks at me.

"What are you
talking about?"

"When I was in the
hot tub.
I was looking at
all the stars.
There were millions!

And I saw Venus.
It's the brightest star.
Except it's not a star.

It's in the western sky.
If we find Venus,
we'll know that's west."

"Yeah? So?"
Sarcastic.
Angry.

"What good does
that do us?"

"The road is west of
the cabin.
Remember yesterday?

When we watched
the sunset
from the cabin's
front porch?

We were facing west.
The road is west
from the cabin."

        She stares at me.
        Says nothing.

        Shakes her head.
        "Unbelievable."

"What's wrong now?"
Now I'm
sarcastic.
Angry.

        Still shaking her head.
        "It's unbelievable
        how stinking,
        freaking
        smart
        you are."

ALL ALONE

I can't keep
from smiling.
Nat doesn't
give me
compliments often.

"Look for the
brightest star,"
I say.

"It's kind of low
in the sky."

We both try to
peer through
all the trees.

Nat tilts her head back.
Looks up at the stars
overhead.

"Those are the
only stars I see, Ab.
I can't see
past the trees."

I slowly turn
in circles.
She's right.
The trees block
our view.

"Keep looking," I say.
My voice sounds
certain.
Confident.

But I feel
a panic rising up
inside me.

Like a rabid animal
ready to
bite.

I see no stars.

I see only
black tree trunks.
Snow glowing blue
in the dark.

My blood freezes
when I realize
we are
all alone.

Lost in the
cold,
dark
night.

SICK, DANGEROUS

My eyes strain
as I keep searching.
Keep turning
in circles.

Hungry for
just a glimpse
of that one lone
bright star.

> "What time is it?
> Do you think
> Mom and Dad are
> back at the cabin yet?
>
> They'll freak when
> we're not there.
> When they see the
> broken glass."

"But we're okay," I say.

Trying to convince myself
as much as her.

"They'll be so happy
when they see we're okay."

"Abby?" Nat says.
Her voice sounds small.

"What if those guys—
what if they went back?

What if they're
lying in wait
for Mom and Dad?"

"They wouldn't do that!"
I yell.
"They're long gone!"

"You don't know that," she says.
"You didn't see the look
in that guy's eyes.
He's sick.
He's dangerous."

Neither of us speaks.

Just one more thing
to worry about.

WE'LL FREEZE

I hear a strange
clacking sound.
I look around.

"Is that you?
Are your teeth
chattering?"

   "A little," Nat says.
   She rubs her hands
   up and down her arms.

   She bounces up
   and down,
   her feet bare
   in the snow.

"Okay.
Time to trade."
I unzip her coat.

Pull Nat's shoes and socks
off my still aching,
tingling feet.

She puts on the coat.
Struggles into her
socks and shoes.

"My feet are
so numb.
Like blocks of ice."

"I know.
We have to
keep moving.
Keep looking
for Venus."

"But which direction
should we go?"

"I don't know.
But if we
don't move,
we'll freeze."

THE BRIGHTEST STAR

Can a person die
from pain
in their feet?

My bare feet
walking through
the snow again
are slowly
killing me.

I want to
lie down.
I want to
curl up in a ball.
I want to
sleep
and sleep
and sleep.

Maybe we can stop.
Just for 10 minutes.
Just till—

"Abby, look!
Up ahead!
The trees are thinner."

Nat's right.
There's a wide stretch of
blue, untouched snow
with only a few trees
around us.

The snow is deeper.
We wade into it.
I search the night sky,

and then I see it.
Above the horizon.

                    The brightest star.

DIAMOND

"That's it!
That's Venus."

I point to the
twinkling light
in the black sky.

Nat stops and stares.

"It's beautiful!
Like a diamond."

I'm so relieved.
We'll be okay now.
We'll be okay.

GOAL

I gaze at Venus
as we walk
toward it.

"As long as
we can keep it
in sight,
we know we're
heading west."

We cross the clearing,
trudging through
the deep snow.

My feet scream
in protest but
I don't listen.

We have a goal now.
Keep walking.
Till Venus leads us
to safety.

TOO FAR

We reach the edge
of the clearing and
we're back among
the tall pines.

It's harder now
to spot
our guiding planet.

But when we lose sight
we stop,
take a few steps,
look
until we find it again.

> "You okay?
> Want my coat again?"

"I'm okay.
For now."

> "Just let me know
> if you get too cold."

How cold
is too cold
I wonder?

How far
is too far
to walk
on a
frozen night?

STRANGE

Something strange

is happening.

My legs are
moving.

I am
moving.

But am I

making them
move?

How is it

that I keep
moving?

How does

my body
know

how to walk?

How

How . . .

DARK WATER

I am swimming
in a pool.
A nighttime pool.

A nighttime pool
at night.

Dark water.
So warm.

Sink
all
the
way
to
the
bottom.

And float.
On the
bottom.
Dark.
Warm.

Pool.
Night.

Abby!
Abby!

Sssshhh.
Let me
float.

OW!

"Ow!" I yell.

Natalie slaps me
again.

Hard on my right cheek.
My left cheek
still stings
from the first slap.

"OW!
Quit
hitting me!"

I am
not standing.
I am in a
crumpled heap.

Not sure
what happened.

"Are you
awake now?"

Nat's leaning over me.
Her nose an inch
from mine.

"Stop hitting me!"

"Stop passing out on me!
You scared me to death."

My head clears
a little.
The dream
of floating
in a pool.

"I didn't pass out!"
I yell.
"I was just—
taking a little
nap."

> *"Listen to me.*
> You cannot
> fall asleep.

> You will
> freeze to death
> if you do.

> We are not
> going to die
> in these woods."

RUN

Natalie grabs me
by both shoulders.
Pulls me to my feet.
Shakes me hard.

"Stop it!
God!
When did you
get so violent?"

    "Just making sure
    you're good and
    awake.

    Here, your turn to
    wear the coat and shoes
    again."

"Just the coat,"
I say.
"The shoes hurt
my feet
too much.
I'm honestly better
without them."

    Amazingly,
    she doesn't argue.
    Or hit me.

She hands over
the coat and
I slip it on.

"You know what
we should do?
We should run.
Really get the blood
flowing."

She grabs me
by the arm and
drags me along.

Through the trees.
Keeping Venus
in sight.

RUNNING TO VENUS

It actually works.

Breathing in cold air.
Pumping my legs.
Pumping my arms.

Gets my heart pumping.
Warms me up.
Clears dreams
and cobwebs
from my head.

I'm running to Venus.
It doesn't feel far.

BLACK RIBBON

It's easier to
spot Venus now.
Not as many trees.

"Is that the road?
Abby, I think
that's the road
up ahead!"

As soon as
Nat says it
I see it.

A black ribbon
running through
the snow.

"It is the road!
Nat, that's it!"

"You were right, Abby!
Go west to the road!"

She runs faster.
I run to catch up
but my feet
aren't working right.

BAM!

I face-plant in
the snow.

NOT THAT FAR

Natalie sees me
and rushes back.

> "Abby!
> Are you okay?
> Are you hurt?"

She helps me sit up.
Brushes wet snow
from my face.

> "Here, let me
> help you."

She grabs my arm.
Throws it around
her shoulders.
Pulls me up
to standing.

> "Come on.
> We'll walk together.
> Just one step at a time.
> It's not that far."

ARM IN ARM

We keep walking
like that.
The two of us.
Arm in arm.

Until we reach
the road.

          "We made it!"
          Nat lets out
          a huge sigh.

The black asphalt
sparkles with frost.

Giant berms of
knee-high snow
run along
both sides of it.

That's from the
snowplows
pushing the snow
aside.
Forming
short walls of
hard, crusty,
frozen snow.

We climb over them.
Stand on the asphalt
and look first one way,
then the other.

WHICH WAY?

Now that we're
finally here,
we're not sure
what to do.

      "Which way
      should we go?"

"I don't know."

      "You don't know?"

I hear the annoyed
surprise in her
voice.

"I don't know, okay?"

      "Can't you
      figure it out?
      Like you did with
      Venus?"

THIS WAY

I look one way,
then the other.

"This way,"
I say.
Pointing to
the right.

"Okay."
Nat seems
satisfied.
She starts walking.

I lag behind.
I feel the cold
of the pavement
from my bare feet
all the way
to my hips.

I'm in frozen pain.
My head feels
fuzzy.

I don't know
the way.
I just picked
one randomly.

I can't think
straight.
My brain's too
cold.

But maybe
this is
the way.

Maybe
it'll be
okay.

ANY MINUTE NOW

Nat is walking fast.
I can't keep up.
I try but I'm walking
with someone else's
feet.

Someone's feet
I can't even feel.

"Nat, wait up!"

   She looks back,
   stops,
   waits for me to
   reach her.

"Listen, let's stop
and rest.
I need to sit down
just for a minute."

   "No! We cannot
   stop!
   Abby, it's okay.
   We'll get help
   any minute now."

"Okay," I say.
We keep walking.

  "Any minute a car
  could drive by."

"Right," I say.
"Any minute."

I want to
sit down.
I want to
lie down.

I want to
lie down
and never
get up
again.

LIGHTS AHEAD

We walk for—
how long?
Five minutes?
Fifteen?

Hard to say.
Time seems so

        distorted.

Then out of
the black
we see them.

Lights ahead!
Coming toward us.

WEIRDEST THING

"Headlights!" we yell
at the exact same time.

It wakes me
out of my fog.

A car is
coming!
We both start
running.

Up the road.
Toward the
headlights.

Waving our arms
over our heads.
So the driver
will see us.

Then the
weirdest thing
happens.
The car
speeds up.
We hear the
engine gunning.

Headlights
barreling
toward us!

Faster. Faster.

ELECTRIC ADRENALINE

For half a second
we stop and stare,
frozen in the beams.

Not believing what
we see.

"Abby, run! Run!"

Nat grabs me,
spins me
so quick
I almost fall.

Electric adrenaline
shoots through me,
and we're
running!

As the speeding car
chases us down.

LAST THING

We barely
make it to
the berm.

Natalie vaults over it
in one leap.
Drags me along
behind her.

I tumble into
the snow
by the side of
the road.

I'm lying there.
Can't move.
The last thing
I see is
Nat running
away from me.

CRASH!

Screaming
               engine sounds
          thundering

CRASH!

Chunks of
frozen snow
fly through
the air.

Smell of
burning rubber
stings my nose.

        I sit up
        and stare.

The car crashed
smack into
the berm.

The engine is
still running.

Two headlight beams
shine into the
dark night.
Lighting up
treetops.

The car is stopped
at a crazy angle.

DARK SHADOW

Wait—
it's not a car.
It's a pickup.

A mud-splattered
pickup.

Driver's door
opens.

I can't move.
Can't scream.
I sit here
paralyzed.

Watch as
a dark shadow
walks toward me.

GOATEE

The shadow gets
closer and
I get a better look
at him.

Goatee.

He climbs over
the smashed-up berm.
Trudges through
the snow.

He comes toward me
and
instead of moving,
instead of running,
all I can think is,

Sick.
Dangerous.

LOOKING FOR YOU

I glance back
at the pickup
expecting to see
Trucker Hat
coming at me,
too.

He's nowhere
in sight.
Goatee must have
left him behind.

Goatee walks up,
stands over me.
He leans down
and chuckles.

A dry, sandpapery
laugh that
chills my blood.

"Well, whatta ya know?
I been looking for
you girls all night."

SNAKE EYES

Why can't I move?
I'm frozen here.
Staring back
at him as he
grins his evil grin
at me.

First time
I've gotten a
really good look
at him.

Seen him
up close.
He's greasy,
skinny,
with ink
on his cheek.

A pair of dice.
(What's that
called?)

Oh yeah.
Snake eyes.

ME HE'S AFTER

I see an angry red
gash on his neck.
Splotches of
dried blood on
the gray T-shirt
under his jacket.

So I really did
stab him with
the icicle.

Good!

But not enough
to stop him.

Because
here he is.

Again.
And this time,
it's me he's after.

AT LEAST

At least
Natalie got away.
At least
Natalie saved herself.

She'll get to safety.
She'll tell Mom and Dad
what happened.

I wait for him
to grab me.
Drag me to his truck.
Drive away with me
into the night.

He's enjoying this.
He crouches
in front of me.

"So you're the
feisty one, huh?
Think you're
pretty smart.

Stabbing me
like that and
running off.

Where's your sister?
She took off.
Left you.
Looks like
it's just you and—"

Thump!

ANOTHER BLOW

Goatee lets out
a grunt.
Slumps over.

A shadow is
behind him.
Raising its arms
for another blow.

Thump!

Goatee falls
face forward.
Lands half
on top of me.

I shove him
off me and scramble
out of the way.

Dark liquid
oozes from
his head,
streams across
the snow.

Natalie stands
over him.
A giant chunk of
frozen snow
as big as a football
is in her hands.

Goatee
lies there
not moving.

I look up
at Natalie.

"I think . . .

I think
you killed him."

STILL

Natalie leans
over him.
I'm too freaked out
to even look.

The back of
my throat burns
as I start to gag.

I clamp my
jaw shut
and try not
to puke.

Millions of thoughts
run through my head.

Self-defense!
He tried to kidnap
both of us!
We had no choice!

Out of the
corner of my eye,
I take a quick glance.

He's absolutely
still.
Not moving.

NOT EVERY DAY

Nat slowly
stands up.

"He's still breathing."

Okay. Okay.
At least we
didn't kill him.

Nat looks around.
"Where's the other guy?"

"He wasn't in
the truck.
Goatee was
all alone."

"Are you okay, Ab?"
She's shaking all over.
Her voice all quivery.

"Yeah, I'm okay.
Are *you* okay?"

It's not every day
my sister and I
both attack a guy
who's trying to
kidnap us.

It's not every day
we turn icicles
and frozen snow
into deadly weapons.

"I am now.
A few cuts on
my hands, though."

She holds them out
and shows me.
The frozen ice
cut them in a few places.

"Ouch, Nat."
I reach for her hands.
They're bleeding a little.
She brushes me off.

"They're fine.
But what do
we do now?"

SAVE OURSELVES

I look at
the pickup,
its front tires
half-buried
in the berm.

Engine
still running.
Headlights
shining into
the dark night.

"We can take
his truck.
We'll drive
into town
and get help."

       Nat's eyes
       get big.
       "I can't drive
       that thing!
       It's huge!"

"Oh, yes you can.
Come on.
This is how we
finally
save ourselves."

SMART

We step over
the unconscious
Goatee.

The pool of blood
around his head
looks like
black oil
against the snow.

As gross as
he looks,
I stop for a second.
Remembering
how he taunted me.

I lean over him.
"One last thing,"
I say.

He lies there
unmoving.

"I don't think
I'm smart.
I know
I'm smart."

WARM

We climb over
the berm and
head for the truck.

"I'm not sure
I can drive this,"
Nat says.

"You can.
Just take it
slow."

We get inside
the cab.
It stinks from
cigarettes and
body odor.

Pile of trash
on the floor.
I curl my frozen feet
under me so
I won't touch it.

It takes Natalie
a few minutes to
figure out where
everything is.

Her feet can't reach
the pedals, so
she adjusts the seat.

The heater is blasting
hot air.
I let out a sigh.

For the first time
all night
maybe I can finally
get warm.

STUCK

Nat puts the truck
in reverse and presses
on the gas.
The tires spin.

But we don't move.
I watch dirty chunks
of snow spew out
in front of the headlights.

She's looking at me,
biting her lip.
That's her
nervous face.

    "We may be stuck," she says.

"Try it again," I say.

Nat presses on
the gas harder.
Same thing.

Spinning tires.
Flying snow.
But no
movement.

    "We're stuck," she says.

"Keep trying," I say.

"I am trying!
We're not moving!"

"Try harder!" I yell.
"Stomp on
that pedal!"

The engine roars,
the truck jerks
backward.

Bounces off
the berm in a
hard jolt.

Nat slams on
the brakes.

We both stare
in shock
at each other,
and then

we burst out
laughing.

SLOWLY

"Nice job!" I say.

    "Now what?" she asks.

I stretch my hand out
toward the road
ahead of us.

"Now drive. Just—
drive."

    She takes a deep breath.
    "Okay. I got this.
    I think."

Carefully,
she shifts
into drive.

Then
slowly
slowly
she pulls out
onto the
dark road.

We creep along.

S l o w l y.

We're both silent
as
we
roll
down
the
road.

Going
about
six
miles
an
hour.

Finally, I break
the silence.

"I might get out
and walk
for a bit.
Just to get there
faster."

Nat reaches over
and slaps me hard.
(This new violent streak
of hers continues.)

But she can't stop
laughing
either.

DAD'S DRIVING LESSONS

Gradually she
speeds up
a little.

"I'm nervous," she says.
"There's a foot of snow
everywhere.
I'm driving a tank.
This is really scary."

There may be snow
on the ground, but
at least the road is clear.

"How are your hands?"
I ask.

She loosens her
death grip on
the steering wheel
for a second.
Looks at one palm.

"They're okay.
A little sore.
Not bleeding anymore."

"That's good.
And you're doing
a great job driving,"
I tell her.

She's only had
her license since
last fall.

She's still an amateur.
If it were up to her,
she'd never drive.

But Dad makes her
practice.
"Thank God for all
Dad's driving lessons,"
I say.

He's always saying
he wants us to be
strong, independent.

I can't wait for him
to hear what we've done.

LET ME FINISH

"By the way,"
I say.
"Thanks for
saving my life
back there."

She lets out
a nervous laugh.

> "We saved
> each other, Abby.
> I can't believe you!
> You are *so smart*.
> Hiding in the
> hot tub so they
> didn't catch you.
> Stabbing Goatee
> with the icicle.
> Speaking Tagalog!"

"That part
I didn't plan . . ."

> "Shut up and let me finish.
> And since when
> did you become
> an astronomer?
> I mean, how did
> you know that
> about Venus?"

My face feels warm.
From the blowing heater
and all of Nat's compliments.

AMAZING

She glances over,
looking at me like
she's never
seen me before.

"You really are
amazing,
you know that?"

Amazing.

She keeps
looking at me,
and
I don't know
what to say.

I have a
big, stupid
smile
on my face.

I just
love my sister
so much.

"Thanks," I say.

It comes out
squeaky.

IT SAVED US

"You're pretty amazing, too.
And you're right.
We saved each other."

I slump down
in the seat.
I could
fall asleep
right now.

But I make myself
stay awake.
The whole
crazy night
swirls through
my head.

I really am smart.
I analyzed the situation
and didn't panic.

I was logical
about everything.

But mostly,
I actually
did something.

I tend to
overanalyze.
Think of
a million
different solutions,
but then
I don't
act on them.

But tonight
I did.

And it saved us.

RIGHT DIRECTION

I glance out
the windshield
and see lights
in the distance.

Lights from
the town.
Whew.

So we've been
going in the
right direction.

Toward civilization
instead of farther
outside of town.

Nat reads my mind.

"What should we
do when we get to town?"

I shrug.
"I guess stop
at a convenience store
or something.
Go inside and
ask them to
call 911.

Then we'll
get in touch with
Mom and Dad
and let them
know we're okay."

Natalie nods.
Bites her lip.
But this time
with a look
of determination.
Not worry.

"Good idea.
Sounds like a plan."

SPEECH

Our night of
danger
and adventure
is almost
over.

And I'm starting
to feel—
almost a little
sad
that it's
coming to
an end.

This is
the closest
I've felt
to my sister
in a
long
long long
time.

So—
I start to
plan
this little
speech
in my head.

Things I want
to say to her.
Things I want
her to hear.

BUT THEN

But then

I don't.

Because words
aren't my thing
really.

And I'll never say
what I mean to say.

So instead

I say this.

NO MORE FIGHTING

"You know what?
I promise
I'm not going to
fight with you.
Ever again.

We've got
eight more months
together
before you leave
for college.

We have to
make the
most of it."

Natalie bursts out
laughing.

"Are you serious?
No more fighting, ever?
You really think
we can go eight months
and not fight?"

"You're right.
I take that part back.
We're definitely
going to keep fighting.
Maybe even in
the next ten minutes."

171

That makes us
both laugh.

We ride on
in silence.
Getting closer
to the lights.

> "One thing
> I know for sure, Ab.
> You've always
> got my back.
> And I've got yours."

Staring at the road
ahead,
she reaches over
and takes
my hand.
Which is a
big deal.

Not the
hand-holding.
We did that
all the time
when we
were little.

I smile at
my sister,
nervous driver.
Letting go
long enough
so she can
hold on to me.

MY POOR FEET

My poor feet,
those frozen
blocks of ice,
are killing me
again.

I've been sitting
with them
curled under me.

The warmth
from the heater
and
from my legs
is starting to
thaw them out.

And they're
screaming in pain.

I sure hope I
don't have
frostbite.

Is the fact
that they're
hurting
a good sign?

At least
I've still got
feeling in them?

I hope so.

I'm sure
Mom and Dad
will want to
take us to
urgent care.

Get us checked out.
Make sure
we're okay.

And for once,
I won't argue
with them.

I know we're
mostly okay,
but better to
be sure.

IN TOWN

We're now driving
into town.
The streetlights
seem crazy bright.
Make us blink.

Nat lets go of
my hand,
grips the
steering wheel
tight.

"I'm pulling in here,"
she says.
Nodding toward
the gas station
on the right.

She pulls in.
Then carefully
carefully
eases into
a parking space.

She fumbles
with the gear shift
till she gets in
park.

Then turns off
the engine.

Silence fills the cab.

Stunned, we sit here
staring at each other.

"Nat, we made it,"
I say.
"We're safe."

NOT YET

Nat opens the
driver's door
and is about
to climb out.

Suddenly,
I lean over her
and pull
the door
shut again.

> "What are you doing?"
> she yells.
> That edge in her voice
> I know so well.

"We'll go inside
in a second,"
I say.
"But not yet.

I just want . . .
I want to say
one more thing."

EVERYTHING

I can tell
she's not
in the mood,
but I don't care.

"It's kind of
corny,"
I start off.

   "Okay."

"But just listen
for a second."

   "Okay."

I take a deep breath.

"We're not just sisters, Nat.
No matter how much
we fight,
you're still
my best friend.

And you always
will be.
Forever.

It's like Mom
always says.
Family is everything."

CORNBALL

Nat is giving me
this intense,
serious
look.

She reaches over,
puts both her hands
on my shoulders.

"Abby, that was so . . .
so

ridiculously corny.

We had the
perfect vibe going
but then you
ruined it all
with that
total
cornball move."

I'm laughing.
She's laughing.
We're hugging.
And we're
safe.
Warm.
Okay.

LET'S GO

I stare at the
glass front of
the gas station.

See the cashier
behind the counter.
Young guy,
maybe twentysomething,
looking sleepy
and bored.

A few random
customers.
Otherwise,
it's quiet.

"Okay," I say.
"Let's go."

TOGETHER

We open our doors
and climb out of
the giant cab
of the pickup.

All night
I've trudged through
the snowy woods
wearing a swimsuit
and a hoodie.

My aching bare feet
feel the cold of
the pavement.

I take off Nat's coat
and wrap it around
my waist.

Nat walks around
the front of the truck.
She's standing there
waiting for me.

We grab
each other's hands
and walk through
the glass doors
into the dazzling lights.

Together.

DRIVING HOME

Our family is
in our car
driving home.

The afternoon sun
streams in through
the windows.

What a crazy night!
Our first 911 call.
Mom and Dad both cried
when they saw
we were safe.

The cops found Goatee
where we left him and
took him into custody.

I have "superficial frostbite"
but no permanent damage.
(It'll take months
to heal, though.
Ouch.)

Mom's realtor friend Steve,
the cabin's owner,
plans to install a
major security system.

After sleeping all morning
in a hotel,
we are finally
driving home.

Mom and Dad
tell us we are
      brave,
      smart,
      resourceful.

Not even sure
what they mean
by that last word.

BONDED

Nat and I
are in the back seat
barely awake.
She moves over,
leans her head on
my shoulder.

We are bonded
by so much.
Our blood.
Our whole childhoods.
Last night's terror.

We sometimes
pull apart.
We sometimes
fight.
We sometimes
spend no time
together.

But

I feel closer to
Nat now
than I've felt
in a long time.

Will it last?
I think so.
Hope so.

No—
I know so.

WANT TO KEEP READING?

If you liked this book, check out another
book from West 44 Books:
THREE SHOTS
BY KATY GRANT

ISBN: 9781978596535

Three Shots

rang out
during the night
while I slept not
knowing.

One-two.
Three.

Those three shots
ended three lives.
Broke many hearts.
Hurt more people
than I can count.

Shattered

my

world

forever.

Three Days Before

Everything was normal.
I thought.

Friday after school,
I text my friend Gracie,
            Down for a street sesh?

                        YES! Always, she answers.

So I grab my board and
head to our meet-up spot.
Halfway between our houses.
First week in November.
Perfect weather.
Sunny, 80 degrees.
Not too hot.
The long
            long
                        long desert summer
finally over.

Gracie comes pushing down the street.
Nollies over a dead palm frond.
"Dope!" I yell.

> She looks up, laughs.
> "Le's getit!"
> She's slim, athletic.
> Sun-streaked hair
> falls out of a ponytail.
> T-shirt sleeves rolled up
> like always.

The thing about skating street is
just the fun of looking for
all that's skateable.
Finding the challenge.
Being creative.

Nothing like spotting an obstacle
a little too high, kinda awkward.
Maybe has a lousy run-up.
Scoping how you'll hit it.

Skating only parks you get lazy.
Every ledge, rail, box waxed buttery.
So on days like today, you go
prowl for some new spots
you're gonna want to skate
forever.

Street Sesh on a Friday

We're flowing the streets.
Landing flatground tricks.
Heel flips, pop shuv-its,
the *whir whir whir* of
wheels skimming hot asphalt.

Gracie's always progressing.
Today it's a
no-comply 180 nosegrab.
"First try?" I say.
"First try!" she says.

She then misses it
five, six, seven …
"You're this close," I say.
"I gotta commit," she says.

CHECK OUT MORE BOOKS AT:
www.west44books.com

WEST **44** BOOKS™

ABOUT THE AUTHOR

Katy Grant is the author of ten novels for young readers, including *Three Shots* and *Disaster Trail*. For many years, she taught creative writing and composition courses at the college level. A native of Tennessee, she now lives in northern Arizona with her husband. She enjoys travel, hiking, biking, and spending time with her two adult sons.